Samuel French Acting Edition

I0591758

Vérité

by Nick Jones

SAMUELFRENCH.COM   SAMUELFRENCH.CO.UK

FOR PRODUCTION ENQUIRIES

UNITED STATES AND CANADA
Info@SamuelFrench.com
1-866-598-8449

UNITED KINGDOM AND EUROPE
Plays@SamuelFrench.co.uk
020-7255-4302

Each title is subject to availability from Samuel French, depending upon country of performance. Please be aware that *VÉRITÉ* may not be licensed by Samuel French in your territory. Professional and amateur producers should contact the nearest Samuel French office or licensing partner to verify availability.

MUSIC USE NOTE

VÉRITÉ was first produced by the LCT3/Lincoln Center Theater in 2015. The performance was directed by Moritz von Stuelpnagel, with sets by Andrew Boyce, costumes by Paloma Young, sound by Stowe Nelson, original music by Ryan Rumery. The Production Stage Manager was Amanda Michaels. The cast was as follows:

JO DARUM	Anna Camp
LIZ DARUM	Jeanine Serralles
JOSH DARUM	Danny Wolohan
LINCOLN DARUM	Oliver Hollmann
ANDREAS VENLER	Matt McGrath
SVEN KANDETTY	Robert Sella
WINSTON	Ebon Moss-Bachrach

CHARACTERS

JO DARUM – female, mid-thirties, prone to nervousness
LIZ DARUM – mid-thirties, brash
JOSH DARUM – male, early forties, means well but easily irritated
LINCOLN DARUM – boy, eight years old, dry delivery
ANDREAS VENLER – male, early thirties, Norwegian
SVEN KANDETTY – male, mid-thirties, Norwegian
WINSTON – male, late twenties/mid-thirties

The total cast size is seven: two female, five male (including one youth).

SETTING

Patterson, New Jersey
New York City
Bogota, Colombia

TIME

2015

AUTHOR'S NOTES

Punctuation Note: A "/" indicates overlapping dialogue.

1.

(Patterson, New Jersey. A cramped attic apartment.)

(JO is in bed with her seven-year-old son, LINCOLN. Her husband JOSH is seen sitting nearby. She reads from a printed manuscript.)

JO. "...Phaemora gripped the dragon tighter as it swooped in low over the treetops. Straight toward the burning castle!

Stop, Hargor, stop. You know humans are not immune to flames like dragons.

But it was no use. They were diving now, into the smoke...

Phaemora closed her eyes tight, bracing herself. Was this how it would end? Now, after all she'd been through? After crossing the Forest of Slumber, and the Gates of Smee. After Arnold's Pendulum, and the Fiery Lake of Boog.

Suddenly Phaemora hated that wizard. For filling her mind with such a silly notion. Who was she to think she could save the realm? She was not a hero. She was just a simple farm dwarf. But it was too late to turn back. And somewhere behind this wall of smoke was a magic chalice with the power to make everything right again."

(Puts it down.)

End of chapter twenty-two.

LINCOLN. Why's it a chalice? I thought it was a magic goblet.

JO. I had to change it.

LINCOLN. Why?

JO. Because in the *Teen Angel* series, they have a big storyline about a magic goblet. Though goblet sounds better, doesn't it?

> (**LINCOLN** *shrugs.*)

It does, it sounds better...

JOSH. Why can't you both have magic goblets?

JO. Because then my book will sound derivative.

JOSH. Oh. It's about dragons and dwarves, babe.

JO. What are you saying?

JOSH. Why don't you just call it a magic cup? Why does it have to be all medieval-y?

JO. Because it's set in medieval times.

LINCOLN. They had cups in medieval times.

JOSH. Yeah.

LINCOLN. I think there's probably been cups always.

JOSH. Listen to the man. He knows what he's talking about.

JO. I know, but that's not...that's not the point.

JOSH. Alright alright, what do we know? But if you ask me, just leave it alone. If nobody's published it by now, a little word change isn't gonna make a difference.

JO. Everything makes a difference. And I wish you'd be a little more supportive.

JOSH. I'm taking time off work for this. That's not supportive? Look, all I'm saying is why don't you meet these people and see if they even want to publish your book before you go and start changing everything. Don't waste more time than you already have.

JO. You think this is a waste of time?

JOSH. I mean, because it's already perfect. It's a waste of time trying to improve something that's already perfect. 'Kay?

JO. 'Kay.

JOSH. I'm gonna go see if Liz has any movies I can borrow.

> (**JOSH** *walks out the front door, and down to the lower level of the house where his sister lives.*)

LINCOLN. I think it's really good, mom.

JO. Thank you, sweetie. I love you.

LINCOLN. I love you, too.

JO. Now go brush your teeth.

> (**LINCOLN** *exits, and* **JO** *puts on a jacket, transitioning into…*)

2.

(A New York City publishing office, modest but tasteful.)

(JO, dressed in a winter jacket, is led in by ANDREAS, a sharply dressed man with a hard-to-place accent. It might be Norwegian?)

ANDREAS. Can I take your jacket?

JO. Ah, yes. Well, no, it's alright.

ANDREAS. Mr. Kandetty will be here in just one minute. Sorry to make you wait.

JO. It's okay.

(He sits down across from her, smiling. He seems enchanted with her throughout, without ever letting her feel at ease.)

ANDREAS. So.

JO. So.

ANDREAS. You wrote a novel.

JO. Yes.

ANDREAS. It is quite intriguing.

JO. Oh, you read it?

ANDREAS. Yes, our whole office has read it. That's why you're here.

JO. Oh, wow.

ANDREAS. Yeah, yeah…

(Beat.)

JO. And how did you come across it, if you don't mind my asking?

ANDREAS. We have associates that pass on things they think we'll like.

JO. It's just been a while since I sent it out anywhere.

ANDREAS. Did no one else contact you about the book?

JO. Recently?

ANDREAS. Ever?

JO. No.

ANDREAS. Ah. Well. People are looking for all different things.

    (They nod, through a beat.)

And how long did it take you to write this...novel?

JO. I started it when I was in high school.

ANDREAS. Oh so long time –

JO. I mean, I've stopped and started...

ANDREAS. Of course.

JO. ...when my son was born, I had to put things aside.

ANDREAS. Nothing wrong with taking your time...if it pays off.

JO. Yes. Thank you. *(Correcting.)* I mean, if you're saying...if you think it has paid off.

ANDREAS. Well nobody's paid you anything yet *(Laughs.)*

JO. ...

ANDREAS. Look, I don't want to say much until Sven gets here, but you are very exciting find for us. I am very excited to be talking with you.

JO. *(Pleased.)* Oh...

ANDREAS. And I appreciate the hard time you must have had, as a mother of babies, also trying to make a career as a writer.

JO. Well, even if I can't make a career of it, I love to write. I find it relaxing.

ANDREAS. *("Aren't you cute?")* Relaxing?

JO. Yes.

ANDREAS. Hm. Well...you're at the beginning of your journey.

    (SVEN enters.)

SVEN. Hello.

    (JO stands. Her jacket falls off her lap to the floor. JO and SVEN awkwardly vie to pick it up.)

Please don't stand.

JO. Oh. /Whoops.

SVEN. *(Without going for it.)* I'll get that for you.

JO. No no I have it. Thank you. Thank you.

SVEN. Sorry about that, Jo. Is it alright if I call you Jo?

JO. Yes. It's my name.

SVEN. Ha ha yes it is. Jo. Jo Darum.

ANDREAS. Jo Darum.

> *(They beam at her proudly. Then, remembering there is business at hand:)*

SVEN. Ah well. Please. Sit.

JO. Thank you. I mean…

SVEN. Can we take your coat?

ANDREAS. She wants to hold it.

SVEN. Ohhh. That's alright then. It does get a little chilly in here sometimes. You know these old buildings. Sometimes the heat just runs and runs.

ANDREAS. Runs and runs…

SVEN. So I have to open the window just so I can bear it.

JO. Yes. I… I hate being cold.

SVEN. Oh god. It's just so. It's just the worst, isn't it?

ANDREAS. I hate it. I've always hated it.

SVEN. Why do we live in New York, when it's like this? Oh, goodness sake please…

> *(Small laughs.)*

Did you have any trouble finding us? I know it's hard to see the sign.

ANDREAS. Because there is no sign.

> *(They laugh and* **JO** *laughs along.)*

JO. No, I found you. I just followed your directions from / the email –

SVEN. Well, we're glad you can follow directions.

> *(Beat.)*

ANDREAS. Would you like any water?

SVEN. Oh yes. How rude. Andreas, get Jo some water.

JO. No, please.

ANDREAS. It's no trouble.

JO. No really –

ANDREAS. It's *no trouble*, Jo.

> (**ANDREAS** *opens a cabinet, completely full of bottled water.*)

JO. Okay.

> (**ANDREAS** *offers it to her. She takes it.*)

Thank you.

ANDREAS. For later. You never know when you'll need water. What if the world ends? *(Correcting himself.)* I mean, if there is a tragedy that cuts us off from our water supply ha ha.

JO. Ah.

SVEN. *(Laughingly.)* Andreas. Why are you so morbid all the time?

ANDREAS. I don't know. I just say things sometimes. I feel like I'm basically a happy person, but every so often I say something that *is just so dark* ha ha.

SVEN. Well maybe you should have been a writer. People like to read about dark things.

> *(Laughter.)*

You have a bit of dark streak, don't you, Jo?

JO. Do I?

SVEN. Oooh yes. Your book is very dark. We enjoyed it quite a bit.

ANDREAS. Yes.

SVEN. We love your voice.

ANDREAS. Love it.

JO. Thank you, thank you.

SVEN. And it's very rare you know to come upon a voice that feels fresh.

ANDREAS. Fresh and raw.

SVEN. Raw in a good way.

JO. Thank you.

ANDREAS. You're a natural talent, Jo.

SVEN. You're the kind of talent we dream of finding.

ANDREAS. Finding you is like finding a diamond in the trash.

SVEN. This is what we live for.

JO. Thank you.

SVEN. Yes.

JO. That's so nice.

SVEN. Yes, so it's unfortunate that we can't move forward with this book right now. But don't mistake us. It is so great.

ANDREAS. It's fantastic.

SVEN. But it is, um, a little ennnn…

ANDREAS. Ennn…

SVEN. It feels a bit made up.

ANDREAS. Yeah. So.

> *(Beat.)*

JO. But it is made up. It's about a war between dragons.

ANDREAS. Yes!

SVEN. Yes, exactly!

ANDREAS. That's a problem for us, because we don't like to do books like that.

SVEN. No. No fantasy! I mean, maybe if you like that childish shit, oh dear…

JO. What?

SVEN. I said maybe if our last president was here. He had soft spot for fantasy themes.

ANDREAS. But now we are reality-based company. So to speak.

SVEN. And so to write.

ANDREAS. Ah ha!

SVEN. There may be a kernel of truth in the fiction you write, but we want more than the kernel. We want the whole corn.

ANDREAS. Oh ho!

SVEN. Do you understand?

JO. Yes. But not really. If you're not interested in publishing my book then why did you ask me to come in?

SVEN. Ah ha.

ANDREAS. There it is.

SVEN. We asked you to come in because we want to publish your *next book*. Jo, what do you think about the idea of writing a memoir?

JO. A memoir? About what?

ANDREAS. About your memoir-ies.

> *(They laugh.)*

SVEN. Andreas. You are so stupid. Jo, we have no taste for that thing you write about in *Dragonscape*. But we love your voice.

ANDREAS. Love it.

SVEN. And so we were thinking, what if only she was talking about something *real?*

ANDREAS. What if only she'd let us into her life where the reality is.

JO. Yeah, it's all very flattering, it's just, honestly, I doubt my life is so interesting anybody would want to read about it.

SVEN. No, it isn't.

ANDREAS. Not yet.

SVEN. But the thing is, Jo, what if we *made* your life interesting?

JO. Made it interesting how?

SVEN. Well, that's something we can discuss.

ANDREAS. Or not.

SVEN. The point is: no problem.

ANDREAS. We'd work with you.

SVEN. Look: People come in here with ideas all the time.

ANDREAS. We get non-fiction pitches all day.

SVEN. All day, all night. I go home at night and my wife pitches me and I am like shut up, I have no interest. I don't care about stupid old woman's ideas. I care about writers.

ANDREAS. It's all about the writer.

SVEN. It's all about the voice.

ANDREAS. Anybody can go to Italy and learn to make pizzas.

SVEN. Or live through a Civil War.

ANDREAS. Or be raped.

SVEN. Or be raped and live to tell about it. But very few select have a voice that is captivating enough so we want to hear about such stuff.

ANDREAS. You have that voice.

JO. Excuse me? "Be raped"?

SVEN. Ah yes, that is funny story. Well not funny like ha ha, but…

ANDREAS. One of our other clients –

SVEN. She was raped –

ANDREAS. Lived to tell about it –

SVEN. Then wrote *Marchers in the Fog*.

ANDREAS. Ten weeks on the best seller list.

SVEN. So in the end, not a funny story, but ultimately profitable for everyone.

JO. *(Offended.)* I'm sorry, but this is not…

> (**JO** *stands to go.* **SVEN** *and* **ANDREAS** *act concerned, talk over her.*)

ANDREAS. Jo…   **SVEN**. Jo, Jo… What?

JO. …This is not the kind of thing I am interested in…

SVEN. There must be   **ANDREAS**. What? What is it?
some misunderstanding.   What kind of thing?

JO. I don't know. I don't know what you're implying.

*(***SVEN*** *and* **ANDREAS** *speak briefly amongst themselves in Norwegian – I guess it's Norwegian for acting purposes, but it should never feel totally clear.)*

SVEN. Hva er galt? *(What's wrong?)*

ANDREAS. Hun er opprørt. *(She's upset.)*

SVEN. Jo, so sorry. We are not being clear.

ANDREAS. It is our English.

SVEN. We want to give you fifty thousand dollars.

ANDREAS. Yes.

JO. For what?

ANDREAS. For your story.

SVEN. Just an advance. To show we're serious about working with you.

JO. That's a lot of money. I'm completely unknown.

SVEN. We know.

ANDREAS. That's what makes it so exciting.

SVEN. Jo, we think you can write the next *Autumn Fire.*

ANDREAS. The next *Mr. Tommerton's Horse.*

SVEN. *The Sad Orderly.*

ANDREAS. *Bobby's Eye.*

SVEN. *The Grabby Friend.*

ANDREAS. *Marchers in the Fog 2.*

*(***ANDREAS** *hands* **JO** *a brochure, and a catalog.)*

Here. About our company. And this is our catalog. You should look this over because we don't have website that is on ordinary internet.

JO. Okay, but if I signed up with you, you wouldn't be, actually be, like, *making things happen to me?*

ANDREAS. What?

SVEN. What? No!

ANDREAS. No! Not ideally.

SVEN. We'd rather you come up with the story.

JO. And what's the story?

SVEN. Whatever you want.

ANDREAS. As long as it's interesting.

JO. Meaning *what*??

SVEN. Meaning don't you think you can make interesting
things come out of fifty thousand dollars? This is
money that is just beginning but this is money to make
dreams come true.

ANDREAS. Or a nightmare.

SVEN. Whatever you want!

JO. What?

SVEN. *(Continuous.)* ...but look Jo, we understand this is big
decision.

ANDREAS. We don't expect an answer right now this
moment.

SVEN. You should talk it over with your husband Josh.

ANDREAS. Josh Darum.

JO. How do you know my /husband's name?

SVEN. We know many things, Jo. And we care deeply about
the writers we work with. Well, I do, anyway. I don't
know about this one.

> *(He gestures to* **ANDREAS***, laughing, like "keep an
> eye on this one." They both laugh, coming forward
> to shake* **JO***'s hand.)*

It is huge joy to meet you, Jo. I look forward to hearing
from you soon.

ANDREAS. Me too. Here. Take more waters for the train.

> *(***ANDREAS*** hands her several additional bottles of
> water.)*

3.

(Back home. **JO** *is looking at the brochure.)*

JOSH. How much?

JO. Fifty thousand.

JOSH. Just to do whatever you want?

JO. As long as I write about it.

JOSH. Holy shit.

JO. As long as it's "interesting."

LIZ. Well, what does that mean?

JO. I don't know.

LIZ. Jo, that's fantastic. Congratulations.

JOSH. It's incredible. So great. I knew you could do it.

JO. It's not, though. I don't know.

JOSH. You don't know what?

JO. I don't know if I want to work with them. I got a bad feeling. It felt like they were…intimating things.

LIZ. Things like what?

JO. Like they'd interfere with the story.

LIZ. Well that's what an editor does.

JOSH. Yeah, you've got to be willing to take suggestions.

LIZ. That's what it means to be a professional.

JOSH. You have to be willing to compromise.

JO. It's more than that. It's hard to explain, but they're not right. I don't want to do it.

LIZ. What's not /right?

JO. Hey Lincoln. Who's that?

> *(Going to greet* **LINCOLN** *as he enters, holding a toy army action figure.* **JOSH** *and* **LIZ** *share a look.)*

LINCOLN. He's a CIA interrogator. He's extracting information from this dolphin.

LIZ. Jo, look, I know you get anxiety, but come on. This is what you've been waiting for.

JO. No, it's not. I don't want to do it. They gave me a bad feeling.

JOSH. And what, you think driving a bus around the Newark airport gives me a *good feeling*? No. That's what the *money's* for! It's called working a job…

JO. Josh! Lower your voice.

JOSH. *(Continuous.)* You think I want to live in my sister's house forever?

LIZ. Hey!

JOSH. Is that what you want? Huh?

JO. Josh, lower your voice. I'm not talking to you when you yell.

LIZ. Yeah, Josh, stop. You're welcome to stay as long as you want.

JOSH. I don't want to stay here.

LIZ. Why? Is it still too cold?

JOSH. No. It's fine.

LIZ. What is it, the toilet? I told you I'm dealing with it. You just need to jiggle the handle.

JOSH. *(Imploring.)* Babe, this is what you've been waiting for.

JO. I don't know. I don't even know if I can write another book. It took me years to finish *Dragonscape.*

JOSH. I know.

JO. It was hard.

JOSH. I know. And it was hard for everyone. Having to hear about it.

JO. What?

JOSH. I said let's just be clear about it: it's not like people are busting down the door. When is another chance like this going to come along?

JO. I don't know.

JOSH. I mean, you always wanted to be published.

LIZ. And we were just saying…

JOSH. Yeah, we were just saying how you should get a real job now that Lincoln's in school.

LIZ. This is even better.

JOSH. And we can use the money.

JO. I know.

JOSH. So. If it means being interfered with, so be it. You have to be a team player.

LIZ. That's right. Jo, I know these kind of people seem shady. And they probably are. But that doesn't mean you shouldn't work with them.

JO. Maybe if we got a lawyer.

JOSH. Of course we'll get a lawyer.

LIZ. Yeah of course get a lawyer.

JOSH. Yeah what are we stupid. Yeah, obviously. But don't turn down an opportunity because of a feeling.

LIZ. No.

JOSH. This is what you always wanted.

LIZ. It's a blessing.

JOSH. It's a blessing. 'Kay?

JO. 'Kay.

JOSH. Don't look a Trojan horse in the mouth.

    (Off her look.)

What?

JO. Gift horse.

JOSH. Huh?

JO. The expression is don't look a gift horse in the mouth. A Trojan horse is full of men who jump out and kill you.

JOSH. Well, either way. For fifty thousand bucks.

4.

(Back in the publisher's office.)

SVEN. Jo.

ANDREAS. Jo.

SVEN. We were beginning to think you had cold feet.

ANDREAS. She probably does have cold feet. It's so freezing out there.

JO. Sorry I'm late. I thought you would cancel, with all the snow.

SVEN. No, we never cancel. We love to work.

ANDREAS. Workaholics!

(They laugh.)

JO. Right. Anyway, it was hell getting in. All the trains were delayed between Patterson and the city. And they cancelled the schools.

SVEN. Oh no!

ANDREAS. No! Don't cancel the schools!

SVEN. So where is Lincoln then?

JO. Oh you know Lincoln?

SVEN. Yes of course. Lincoln.

ANDREAS. Lincoln Darum.

JO. My sister-in-law is watching him.

SVEN. Oh. We were hoping to meet him.

JO. Yes well I think this would be rather boring for him –

ANDREAS. We think it's great you have a son.

SVEN. It makes you more three-dimensional as a character.

ANDREAS. We're hoping Lincoln will be a big part of your memoir.

JO. I'm sure he will be. How could he not be?

SVEN. Absolutely. But that's up to you. Hopefully, our audiences will respond to the others.

JO. The others?

SVEN. *(Ignoring the question.)* Now we spoke to your attorney. Mr Rutenberg. He sent over his little amendments. All fine. We give you little more of movie rights.

ANDREAS. No problem.

SVEN. Obviously we want to retain some stakes, in case the book is big hit.

ANDREAS. Oh yes. Where would we be without the movies?

SVEN. One of only things keeping us going.

ANDREAS. Not that we cater to it. But obviously we do look for stories that have commercial potential.

JO. Of course. It's a business.

ANDREAS. It *is* a business, that's right. But the artist comes first.

SVEN. No matter what happens, this is your story. We're just here to help shepherd it along and help shape it into something anyone would want to read.

JO. Yes, well, thank you for that.

SVEN. You're welcome. Thank you for having your tremendous talent.

　　　　(A beat.)

JO. So, in terms of the story, I want you to know, I'm basically open to anything, so if there's a story you're envisioning…

ANDREAS. Oh. Well…

SVEN. We can't tell you how to live your life.

ANDREAS. I mean we do have ideas…

SVEN. But we don't want to…

ANDREAS. Yeah, we would rather see what you do first.

SVEN. The question is, what do you want?

JO. To say?

SVEN. To say. To do. To be.

JO. I think I'm being it.

　　　　(They look at her. Kind, skeptical, but patient.)

SVEN. Mmmmm. Are you?

JO. Yes.

     *(**SVEN** refers to a document in a yellow binder.)*

SVEN. Hmm.

ANDREAS. Interesting.

SVEN. Married out of high school. Living in the same town you grew up in.

JO. With a wonderful husband and a wonderful son.

SVEN. I agree. They seem very wonderful.

JO. *(Re: the document.)* What is that?

ANDREAS. But will they be compelling to an international audience?

SVEN. Ah ha.

ANDREAS. Don't answer.

SVEN. We're not interested in pandering.

ANDREAS. We're interested in serving the artist.

SVEN. And if you're happy, we're happy.

ANDREAS. There's no reason a happy book won't sell.

SVEN. But as you begin your memoir, I think it's important to consider two things: what you want, and what your audience wants. And then try to strike a balance between the two. Or sacrifice one to the other.

ANDREAS. Like a cow.

SVEN. That's right, like a big fat cow. But look, we'll be here to help you. And we're sure anything you write will be great.

ANDREAS. *(In Norwegian.)* Selv om den er utrolig bra, kan den være dårlig. Hvis den ikke er sann *(But even if it's great, it may be wrong. If it's not truthful.)*

SVEN. Ah yes. Thank you, Andreas. That is very important.

ANDREAS. The *most* important thing.

SVEN. Everything you write about in your book must actually have happened to you. You understand? People will be watching.

JO. Who's watching?

ANDREAS. Everyone.

JO. Watching me?

SVEN. They're watching us, we're watching you.

ANDREAS. Everyone's watching everyone.

SVEN. All those scandals. Those fake memoirs...

ANDREAS. *Dog Run.*

SVEN. *Wiggle Room.*

ANDREAS. *A Quiet Whisper.*

SVEN. *Chores of Desire.*

ANDREAS. *Urban Cannibal.*

SVEN. *Slumping Towards Heaven.*

ANDREAS. *The Humility Contest.*

SVEN. *Pinot Grigio Tears.*

JO. Are those real books?

ANDREAS. No, they were fake!

SVEN. Fortunately, we didn't publish them. We've been lucky to be avoiding big scandals, but only because we're so diligent in fact checking.

ANDREAS. We are small company but number one in fact checking.

SVEN. We believe art should only say truth.

ANDREAS. So long as it's interesting.

SVEN. Obviously. But I think the truth is always interesting.

ANDREAS. Unless everyone hates it.

> (*They laugh.*)

SVEN. Oh god, Andreas, you crack me up. Well let's get on with this, shall we? Unless you have more questions...?

> (**JO** *pushes her questions deep down.*)

JO. No. No questions. I'm a team player.

SVEN. My advice: just relax and have good time with this.

> (**SVEN** *gives her a pen to sign the contract that* **ANDREAS** *slides before her.*)

I know we will.

(**JO** *signs as they smile at her.*)

SVEN. *(Cont.) (Quietly.)* Wonderful.

ANDREAS. *(Quietly.)* Wonderful.

(*She puts down the pen and* **SVEN** *and* **ANDREAS** *look at the signed contract.*)

SVEN. Just first of many beautiful words you will write for us.

ANDREAS. Absolutely. Now just make beautiful initial here. And we begin.

(**ANDREAS** *hands the form back and* **JO** *initials. Then we transition back to...*)

5.

(Home. **JO** *sits among a pile of books, which she has taken from a cardboard shipping box.)*

JOSH. I have an idea. Why don't we go to Myrtle Beach?

JO. Myrtle Beach?

JOSH. Why not? Billy's always going off on how great it is. And Lincoln's got his break coming up.

JO. Why Myrtle Beach?

JOSH. Why not? Don't you want a colorful backdrop for your book? How 'bout it, Link, you want to go to the beach?

LINCOLN. No.

JOSH. Sure you do. You love the beach.

LINCOLN. Okay.

JOSH. Thatta boy.

JO. No, Josh. My memoir is not going to be about a week on Myrtle Beach.

JOSH. Why not? You like the beach.

JO. Yes, I like the beach, but I wasn't given this money just to have a good time. It's not interesting enough.

JOSH. *(With exaggerated patience.)* Fine, fine. Where do you want to go?

JO. I don't know. What do you think about the south of France?

JOSH. The south of France??

JO. Why not?

JOSH. Well for one thing, we don't speak French. For another, we could go to Myrtle Beach and it would be just as nice, and cheaper.

JO. It wouldn't be the same.

JOSH. Alright. How 'bout this: We go to Myrtle Beach, we have a good time, and you write like you're in France?

JO. No.

JOSH. Why?

JO. Because it has to be the truth. They said that.

JOSH. Like they're really going to know…

> (**JOSH** *looks at the box of books.*)

What's all this?

JO. Books my editors sent over.

JOSH. Why? To show you what kind of book they want?

JO. I don't know. Maybe. Or maybe to show me what's already been done, and I shouldn't do?

JOSH. *(Looking at a title.)* Somehow I don't think you're going to write the next *Ghetto Rainbow.*

JO. I know. I wish I grew up in the ghetto. Well, I mean, obviously I'm grateful I didn't, but it would be so helpful. Just so I had something to write about.

JOSH. You have plenty to write about. You were homecoming queen.

JO. No. Nobody wants to hear about that. It needs to be something extraordinary. My life has been predictable.

JOSH. You think so? I would've predicted something better for us than this. Might as well live in the ghetto. At least I wouldn't be paying rent to my sister.

JO. It's not that bad. And it's temporary. If everything goes well with this book, we can get our own place again.

JOSH. Yeah maybe. Too bad you don't know what the fuck you're doing.

JO. What?

JOSH. What?

JO. I don't know what the fuck I'm doing?

> (**JOSH** *sighs. She's always mishearing things.*)

JOSH. Jo. I don't know what this duck is doing…in the sink.

> *(He pulls out a duck toy from the sink.)*

LINCOLN. That's mine. I was waterboarding him.

JOSH. Jesus Christ, Jo. I would never say something like that.

*(**JOSH** walks to the kitchen and begins to prepare sandwiches. **JO** continues to look at the books.)*

JO. I'm sorry. I feel like I'm losing my hearing.

JOSH. Or your mind.

*(It's unclear if he actually said that. **JO** considers responding, but thinks against it.)*

JO. I'm just stressed out.

JOSH. It's fine. You want a sandwich?

JO. Yes. Thank you.

LINCOLN. Why are you stressed out, mommy?

JO. Because this book could lead to other things.

LINCOLN. And that's bad?

JO. No, it's bad if that doesn't happen. If everything stays the same.

LINCOLN. Why is it bad if everything stays the same?

JO. Because it feels good to feel like your life is moving forward. So I have to make sure I do a really good job.

*(**JOSH** returns.)*

JOSH. Look, can I make a suggestion? Why don't we go to Myrtle Beach, and spend some time together as family. There's no point in letting Lincoln's break go to waste and it's been a long time since we went on vacation.

JO. Yeah, I guess.

(The phone rings.)

JOSH. It's just a week. Til you think of something more "interesting."

JO. I guess you're right.

JOSH. I know.

*(**JOSH** picks up the phone.)*

Hello? …Yeah, hold on.

*(To **JO**.)*

It's for you.

(**JO** *takes the phone. We see* **SVEN** *and* **ANDREAS**
in their office.)

JO. Hello.

SVEN. Jo, hello.

ANDREAS. It's Sven and Andreas.

SVEN. How are you?

JO. Uh, good.

SVEN. Just checking in with the book. Want to see if you
have any ideas about where it's headed.

JO. Where it's headed?

ANDREAS. Yeah. How's it going?

JO. It's just been a few days.

SVEN. Yes?

ANDREAS. You mean you haven't started?

JO. No no, of course I've started. I'm working on it right
now.

ANDREAS. Good, but there's no rush.

SVEN. No, though we are hoping to get the book out next
fall.

ANDREAS. Also, Jo, it's very important that your character
makes interesting choices.

SVEN. Yes. Did you get the books we sent you?

JO. Yes.

SVEN. We just thought those might inspire you.

ANDREAS. Because they all feature bold characters making
interesting choices.

SVEN. Interesting choices is the most important thing.

ANDREAS. Well actually that you're truthful is the most
important thing.

SVEN. But that you make interesting choices is the second
most important thing.

ANDREAS. They're both important –

SVEN. The setting is also important. And word choices.

ANDREAS. But mostly just to have fun.

JO. *(Cutting them off.)* Um, excuse me…

SVEN. Yes?

JO. I'm just sitting down to lunch. Would you mind if I called you back?

SVEN. Oh, please…live your life.

ANDREAS. We don't want to get in your way. And obviously all these suggestions are for you to take or throw away.

JO. Of course.

SVEN. In fact, I would even go so far as to say I think you should get away from anyone who is pressuring you to do things you don't want to do.

(**JO** *looks at* **JOSH**.)

But it's up to you.

ANDREAS. Of course.

SVEN. It's your book.

ANDREAS. You're the artist.

(She hangs up.)

JOSH. That was your editors?

JO. Yeah.

JOSH. They're really chomping at the bit to get started, huh?

JO. Champing at the bit.

JOSH. What?

JO. Nothing. Link, come to the table.

(**JO** *goes and draws the blinds as* **LINCOLN** *comes to the table.*)

LINCOLN. What is it?

JOSH. Turkey and cheese.

LINCOLN. *(Disappointed.)* Oh.

JOSH. What? You like turkey and cheese.

LINCOLN. I know. But it's always the same. I like to feel like my life is moving forward.

6.

(A Target-like store.)

(JO and LIZ and LINCOLN push a cart down the aisles.)

LIZ. Stop worrying, it's going to be great. Anyhow, when was the last time you had a vacation?

JO. Well, we went to the Poconos a few summers ago. But that was with your mom.

LIZ. That wasn't a vacation. Do you have a swimsuit?

JO. Assuming I still fit into it.

LIZ. Oh don't worry about it. You'll be the hottest person on the beach. You're a total milf.

JO. Ew.

LINCOLN. What's a milf?

JO. Nothing.

LIZ. No, it's not nothing. It's a compliment. Your mom is a milf, and all of my lady friends are milfs because I have very high standards in friends. Now Lincoln, when you're on the beach you need to wear lots of sunblock and you need to make sure your mom wears it too. Especially on the face and neck. This is where you show your age.

LINCOLN. Okay.

LIZ. Oh you guys are going to have such a good time. I wish I could come.

LINCOLN. Why don't you come, Aunt Liz?

LIZ. *(Considering it.)* Oh you think?

LINCOLN. Come! Come!

LIZ. Oh that would be fun, but…it's better just the three of you…

LINCOLN. Aww.

LIZ. …Besides we have a new girl working at the Bracelet Palace and I don't trust her. When you're a manager, you're responsible for all the people working under you, even if they're lazy or incompetent. But it's an honor. Oh Jo...nuh-uh...

(LIZ takes sunblock out of JO's cart.)

JO. What? What is it?

LIZ. Not this one. This is one of the ones on the bad list. Some of the chemicals in these sunblocks are worse than the sun. It will ruin your face. Here, get this one. This one's alright.

(She gives her another bottle.)

LINCOLN. Mom. Can I get a toy?

JO. No. Not today.

LINCOLN. But what if I just get one, Mom? Mom? What if I just get one?

JO. No.

LIZ. Oh let him get a toy. You're rich now.

JO. No I'm not...and he doesn't need a toy every time we go to the store.

LINCOLN. But I want one. And I don't get one every time we go to the store. I don't get one every time. And they have CIA guys.

LIZ. I'll get it for you. What do you want, baby?

LINCOLN. A CIA guy.

LIZ. Of course.

JO. No, Liz...

LIZ. It's fine.

JO. No...

LIZ. I don't mind.

JO. *(Sharply.)* I don't care if you mind. It's my kid and I said no so just back off!

LIZ. Okay, fine.

LINCOLN. But I want one.

JO. *(Calmer.)* I don't like those kind of toys.

LIZ. I get it. It's fine.

JO. He can get a toy, just please don't –

LIZ. No, whatever you want. It's your kid.

JO. I don't mean it like…he can get a toy, just nothing too violent.

LINCOLN. It won't be.

LIZ. I hear you, loud and clear. We'll meet you at the checkout. Come on, kiddo.

LINCOLN. I want the sniper guy. It's not violent because he does it from far away…

> (**LIZ** *goes off with* **LINCOLN**.)
>
> (**JO** *continues with her shopping.*)
>
> (*A man,* **WINSTON***, approaches. He's in his thirties. He is wearing earbuds, and takes one out as he approaches.*)

WINSTON. Hey there beautiful.

> (*She looks at him, quizzically.*)

Ha ha. Just kidding.

> (*A beat. She takes a step back.*)

Oh, Jo, I'm sorry. I was just kidding. It's me.

JO. You?

WINSTON. Winston?

JO. And I…know you?

WINSTON. We went to high school together. We had AP English with Mr. Callaway.

JO. (*Doesn't remember.*) Oh.

WINSTON. (*Affected voice.*) King Callaway. Cali the Destroyer. Remember?

JO. I remember Mr. Callaway. I never called him that.

WINSTON. Well it was a private joke. I never said it aloud. Are you still writing?

JO. Writing?

WINSTON. I remember you were such a great writer. You used to write about elves and stuff.

JO. (*Touched he remembers.*) Right. Yeah. Wow.

WINSTON. You probably deal with more mature subject matter now I guess.

JO. …

WINSTON. Or maybe you don't. Which is also cool.

JO. No, that was just for fun. Actually, I just signed a book deal for a memoir.

WINSTON. Really? Congratulations. That's fantastic. What's it going to be about? Or should I wait till the movie comes out?

JO. Um, well, actually, I don't know what it's about.

WINSTON. Oh. But you must have written a proposal or something, right?

JO. No. They just gave me the money.

WINSTON. Huh.

JO. Yeah, I know.

WINSTON. Well they must have something in mind. I mean, for fifty thousand dollars.

JO. How do you know it was for fifty thousand dollars?

WINSTON. Huh?

JO. Did I say it was for fifty thousand dollars?

WINSTON. You didn't? You must have. Or how else would I know about it?

JO. I don't know.

WINSTON. Oh right. Right. I ran into Eddie Bruca at the gas station and he told me.

JO. Oh. You know Eddie?

WINSTON. Yeah, I know Eddie, I know Josh, I know all your friends. Because they're also my friends. We all went to high school together? …You really don't remember me?

JO. No.

WINSTON. It's okay. I lost a lot of weight.

(A beat.)

You seem a little stressed out.

JO. I am. It's, uh, the book, just deciding what to...

WINSTON. Oh sure, it's a lot of pressure.

JO. Yeah.

WINSTON. Everyone counting on you.

JO. Yeah.

WINSTON. So much pressure. Crippling.

JO. Right, well...

WINSTON. Well just let things happen as they come.

JO. Right. What else can I do?

WINSTON. What else can you do. Just let things happen as they come and make interesting choices.

JO. Excuse me?

WINSTON. Hey, did you hear about that new bar on Market Street that just opened. I'm going to go down there on Thursday and check it out...

JO. Wait, what did you mean, by making interesting choices? What do you mean by that?

WINSTON. Oh. Well. You know. Like, just make sure everything you do is something that will capture a reader's interest.

JO. And what is that?

WINSTON. If I knew that, I'd have the book deal. But for me, personally, speaking as a reader, I like to read about characters who do things I never would do, because they seem too strange, or dangerous, or counter-intuitive. Because then I'm scared for them, and that's what keeps me turning the pages.

JO. I see. But it's not like I can just deliberately put myself in dangerous situations.

WINSTON. Oh, I'm sure you can do anything you set your mind to, Jo Darum. Hey have you heard about that new bar on Market Street? It sounds really good. I'm going down on Thursday.

JO. Yeah. You said. But I won't be here on Thursday. I'm going to Myrtle Beach.

WINSTON. Oh. Myrtle Beach.

JO. Yeah.

WINSTON. Are you sure that's a good idea? This time of year. Or any time of year? I'm just kidding. Yeah.

JO. You don't think it's a good idea?

WINSTON. No, I was just joking. Mostly. Hey, it's your story. It was really great running into you, Jo. I look forward to reading your book.

7.

(Back home. Bags are packed to leave. **JOSH** *is furious.)*

JOSH. ...A bad feeling? A bad feeling about *what?*

JO. It's just, there's already a book set in Myrtle Beach. It's called *Myrtle Beach.* And it didn't do well.

JOSH. You know what, I can't believe we're having this conversation right now.

JO. I'm sorry, Josh, but I wish you hadn't bullied me into this.

JOSH. Bullied you?

JO. I mean, you didn't even give me a chance to think up something myself.

JOSH. Well it's been two weeks. Do you have a better idea? ...Jo, you're just nervous because you're scared, and you're just scared because everything scares you. We're going to Myrtle Beach. That's the story. Chapter one: right now.

> *(***JOSH*** *takes the bags outside, exasperated.* **JO** *picks up a menu from the table and looks at it.*
>
> *(Alternately: a flyer is suddenly slipped under the door.)*

JO. *(Re: the flyer.)* What is this?

JOSH. What?

JO. Why do they keep leaving these?

JOSH. It's a menu. There's a new place on Market Street.

JO. I know, but why do they keep leaving them?? They've been leaving these all week. Why don't they just leave us alone?

JOSH. It's a new business. They're advertising.

JO. *(A realization)* ...They want me to go there.

> *(A beat.)*

JOSH. Yeah. That's how advertising works.

(A car honks outside.)

Alright, that's us. Lincoln! Time to go!

*(**LINCOLN** enters.)*

JO. I can't. I have to stay.

*(**JO** goes to **LINCOLN**.)*

JOSH. What? Jo... /Don't.

JO. Lincoln, honey, I'm sorry but mommy has to stay home.

LINCOLN. Why?

JOSH. No! Absolutely not! They're non-refundable tickets!

JO. And I paid for them. Because now it's my turn to provide.

JOSH. Oh, so now I'm not a provider...

LINCOLN. Stop yelling!

*(**LINCOLN** runs away.)*

JO. It's alright, honey, we're not...

JOSH. We're not what?

JO. Josh. I need to take this seriously. You're the one who told me I needed to be a team player.

JOSH. This is the team. Not them. Babe, it's your book. You can write about whatever you want.

*(**JO** holds up the menu.)*

JO. Then what's this?

JOSH. Jo, come on.

JO. Nevermind. I can't explain it to you.

JOSH. Because it makes no sense.

JO. Not to you. Because you never thought anyone would want to publish me in the first place.

JOSH. I never said that.

JO. You didn't have to. Look, people are taking an interest in me, Josh. And that is a good thing. For all of us. But it's not going to mean anything unless I can make this worth something. Because I'm sorry, *this, (Gesturing* *around her at the world.*) *this*, is not anything anyone is going to want to read about.

JOSH. Which is why we're going to Myrtle Beach.

JO. NO! NO! Shut up about Myrtle Beach! Shut up about Myrtle Beach! The story is bigger than that. And I think it would be better... I think I would have an easier time figuring out my story if I had some space from you guys for a little while.

LINCOLN. You don't want us in your story?

JO. No, no, of course I do. But it's not about what I want. It's about what's commercial.

LINCOLN. You don't think I'm commercial?

JOSH. What? No! Lincoln, you are very commercial. Jo, tell him. Tell him!

JO. It's not that I don't think you're commercial, it's just that you may not be right for this particular story.

JOSH. Are you kidding me?

JO. My next book will be about my family...

JOSH. Just stop.

JO. ...When I'm with a more literary publisher. Believe me, if it were up to me...

LINCOLN. But I want you to come.

> (JOSH *is shocked. He changes gears, begins ushering* LINCOLN *out of the house.*)

JOSH. Alright. You know what? It's alright...

LINCOLN. No...

JOSH. Mommy needs some space.

LINCOLN. But I want her to come.

JOSH. We're gonna have a great /time without Mommy.

LINCOLN. I want her to come! Mom, I want you to come.

JO. I'm sorry. But part of being a grown up is doing things you don't want to do.

LINCOLN. But I'm not a grown up.

JOSH. It's alright, we'll be fine, just you and me.

LINCOLN. No…

JOSH. It's gonna be great. We'll have a great time. We'll stay up late and eat junk food and do all the things Mom never lets us do.

(*JO tries to hug* LINCOLN *goodbye…*)

JO. I love you, Lincoln.

(*…but he pushes her away, and runs outside.*)

JOSH. *I'm Out of My Fucking Mind.* That should be the name of your stupid memoir.

(*JOSH leaves, slamming the door.*)

(*JO picks up a flyer for the new place on Market Street and looks at it, then we transition to…*)

8.

(The new place on Market Street.)

*(**WINSTON** is sitting at the bar as **JO** enters, apprehensive but knowing, and game.)*

WINSTON. Jo? What are you doing here? What a coincidence.

JO. Is it? I sort of had a feeling you'd be here. Winston.

WINSTON. Really? Oh because I told you I'd be. Yeah, but I thought you were going to Myrtle Beach.

JO. Nevermind that. This is where the universe wants me to be tonight.

WINSTON. *(Not sure how to take that, after a beat.)* Cool. Yeah, I really like this place. It reminds me of places back in my hometown.

JO. I thought this was your hometown.

WINSTON. Right. Good point. That must be why I like it.

JO. So are you meeting someone?

WINSTON. No. Are you?

JO. Meeting you, seems like.

WINSTON. Right. That's funny.

JO. Very funny.

WINSTON. Where's that bartender?

JO. So what is the idea here? Some kind of affair?

WINSTON. What?

JO. It's my husband. I get it. He's not the most likable character when you look at it from the outside. I mean, I like him because I'm used to him. But I can see how an audience would want me to get away.

WINSTON. I have nothing against Josh.

JO. I have nothing against him either. I love him, he's my husband. But that doesn't change the fact that something else is required. Right? Isn't that why we're here?

WINSTON. I guess so.

JO. I'm sorry it's taken me a while to figure out how this works. I hoped I could do it all by myself, but I'm stuck. For whatever reason, I'm stuck, and you have ideas, so I'm just going to... I'm just going to pretend that you're someone I feel comfortable with and you can kiss me.

WINSTON. *(Objecting.)* Okay. Wow...

JO. Please. Now, before I –

WINSTON. Look, Jo, I'll level with you. I *am* attracted to you...

JO. *(Impatient.)* Right, right...

WINSTON. But I don't want to mess up your marriage.

JO. Come on.

WINSTON. Josh is a friend.

JO. No he's not.

WINSTON. Well, we went to the same high school.

JO. No you didn't. I mean you're not in the yearbook, but fine, I won't contradict you. If that's the story, that's the story. Do you want to kiss me or not?

WINSTON. I do. I just didn't think this would happen so fast.

JO. Because I'm behind schedule, and this isn't easy for me. So please don't make it more difficult by...

> *(He kisses her.)*

WINSTON. I just don't want to feel like a homewrecker.

JO. You're not. This is for them. It's all for them.

9.

*(*JO *enters her apartment, quietly, with* WINSTON. *She leads him offstage, toward a bedroom.)*

LINCOLN. *(On answering machine.)* Dragons are real *(Sound of dragon roaring.) (Beep.)*

JOSH. Hey, Jo, it's me. You haven't replied to any of my texts so I'm calling you on the landline. Listen, Lincoln is not – he's not doing so great. I mean, he's fine, it's nothing medical, it's just his mother told him he wasn't commercial and basically made him feel unwanted. So. Dealing with that. But hope you're getting a lot of work done.

*(*JO *stops the answering machine.* WINSTON *enters from the other room.)*

WINSTON. Everything okay?

JO. It's fine. Do you want some coffee or...would you rather just go?

WINSTON. I'll take some coffee.

JO. Okay.

WINSTON. Or I can go.

JO. I'm sorry, it's just strange, all of this, for me.

WINSTON. I understand.

JO. Also, you can't go. Not until my sister-in-law leaves for work. Or she'll see you.

WINSTON. Oh. She lives here?

JO. This is her house. I mean, it's an attic apartment. We have our own entrance but Liz is downstairs.

WINSTON. Right. Liz. Liz Darum.

*(*JO *glances at him for a moment.)*

JO. We lost our house. We couldn't keep up the payments after Josh lost the landscaping business.

WINSTON. He had a landscaping business? Oh right, I knew that.

JO. He's had a lot of businesses, for exceedingly brief periods of time. That's why you're here. But I'd rather not draw attention to this until, well, until the book comes out.

WINSTON. Okay. So…you were planning to write about this then?

JO. Well not just this. I'm expecting more to happen.

WINSTON. Right, but…are you going to change my name?

JO. No, I like your name. It sounds classical.

WINSTON. Thank you, but…then everyone would know that this happened. And you have a son.

JO. I know I have a son. Leave him out of this.

WINSTON. Yeah, I think we should… I wish I knew this was Liz's place, we could have gone to a hotel.

JO. Well, I wasn't thinking. That's not something I ever thought of doing. This is new to me and I can't think of everything all by myself.

> (**JO**, *turning around, knocks a mug off the counter, which shatters.*)

Oh great. Great.

> (*He stoops to help her pick it up.*)

WINSTON. Oh let me help you.

JO. It's alright, I can do it.

WINSTON. Jo, let me help. That's why I'm here.

> (*A moment of reassurance and confirmation. They pick up the mess together. He holds a dust pan or something. It's fumbling but sincere, and for that reason, romantic.*)

JO. Have you done this before?

WINSTON. What?

JO. Introduced a romantic element into a woman's life.

WINSTON. Not in this way. I wouldn't say romance has been my specialty.

JO. Oh no? You work in other genres then?

WINSTON. No, I…what?

JO. It's alright, we don't have to talk about it. We should just play the roles we're meant to play and take it moment to moment. Right?

WINSTON. Right. But…you're not nervous?

JO. Of course I'm nervous. But it's like you said, about characters doing things that scare them. That's important, I think… And that's something I've never done. My whole life I've just tried to avoid things that will hurt me. It's crazy.

WINSTON. You can't avoid getting hurt sometimes. And it teaches you things.

JO. Exactly. I would know so much by now if I hadn't been so protected. And I'm open, you know. I'm open for anything, as long as there's a plan.

(**WINSTON** *looks troubled.*)

WINSTON. A plan?

JO. Yes.

WINSTON. Okay.

JO. What?

WINSTON. Jo, I think I should tell you something. I don't actually live here.

JO. Oh. Really?

WINSTON. Yeah, I was just visiting. I'm leaving in a couple days.

JO. I see. And where are you going?

WINSTON. Bogota.

JO. Columbia?

WINSTON. Yeah, I travel a lot. For my work. They send me all over. I was just passing through.

JO. I see. So I have to go to Bogota.

WINSTON. Oh my god, really? You want to come? I mean you can, if you want to.

JO. It's not about what I want. It's my job.

WINSTON. Either way, amazing. I mean, I'll have some work things to do but we can spend lots of time together –

JO. Does it have to be Bogota though? What about the South of France?

WINSTON. Uh…

JO. Overdone? What about Rio?

WINSTON. My client is in Bogota.

JO. It's alright. If it has to be Bogota, it has to be Bogota. And what do you mean, your client? I'm your client. Your *love client.*

WINSTON. Well I also have a business client.

JO. *(Intrigued.)* Ah because you're a businessman of some kind.

WINSTON. Of some kind. Yeah.

JO. This is the twist I've been waiting for. I knew there was more to you. I knew this would go deeper than a fling. This is good. Bogota. I never would have thought of that.

WINSTON. Wow. Yeah, I was actually thinking of asking you to come, but only in the way you think about doing things you know you'll never actually do.

JO. We have to do those things, Winston. We have to force ourselves to do the things we don't want to do.

WINSTON. You're right. Wow. Oh my god. Jo, can I tell you something else?

JO. Yes?

WINSTON. I didn't just run into Eddie Bruca at the gas station.

JO. Oh wait, wait. Hold on.

> *(She goes and gets a recording device, and turns it on.)*

Just to help me remember. Go on.

> *(WINSTON proceeds, self-consciously at first, as he is aware of being recorded.)*

WINSTON. Um, I didn't just run into Eddie. I called him up, asking about you. I didn't even need to come through town, because my family doesn't live here anymore, but I've always had this…well I guess I think about you. Ah man, this is weird, but…back in the day, I guess I was a little obsessed. I guess in my mind I probably talked to you more than I actually did, which is maybe why you don't remember me. But I…what's, like, love, but sounds less intense? …Well, whatever that is, that's what I had for you. Intensely. I knew you were more special than anyone I had ever met, and more special than anyone gave you credit for. And I could see that. Josh couldn't see that. I always told myself that I'd ask you out, as soon as you guys broke up. But…uh…

JO. But we never broke up.

WINSTON. Yeah. What was up with that?

JO. It's because I was in love. That's been the tragedy of my life, that I met my soulmate too young. And while other people were out there having adventures I've been home stuck with a loving family. That's why I'm boring.

WINSTON. You're not boring.

JO. I am. I could have been out there meeting people like you, meeting all kinds of colorful characters. But it's not too late. And you guys know that.

WINSTON. People say you can't go back. That you can't dwell on the past but I've always felt that's wrong. You can. Because true connections never go away, especially if you haven't made them yet. And love waits.

JO. That could be the title.

WINSTON. It could be. Yes! I knew this would happen someday. I knew that everything else that's happened to me in my life was a mistake, or maybe just dramatic build up to something better. And even though we didn't have so much of a history back in high school, because we were scared to act on our feelings for each other…

JO. Or notice each other.

WINSTON. …Or notice each other, the universe had a plan for us. And this is it. You and me. Right now. And I don't care if it's wrong. I don't care if you write about it and it makes everyone hate me, and I don't care if it sounds intense because I'm an intense guy and I love you. I've always loved you.

JO. Oh my god…

WINSTON. I'm sorry, is that too much?

JO. No. I mean it's overwrought, but that's fine, I'll rework the dialogue.

WINSTON. Do you think I'm pathetic? I can't believe I said all that.

JO. No. No. I love it, Winston. It's beautiful. It's so so good.

WINSTON. Do you remember me?

JO. No, but I will.

> *(She kisses him again, pushing him back on the couch.)*

WINSTON. Ow.

> *(He pulls a plastic action figure from the couch.)*

JO. It's alright, Winston. It's just pain. Live for tomorrow.

10.

(Later that day. **JO** *packs, while dictating into the recorder.)*

JO. "Winston cried out. Lincoln's action figure was digging painfully into his back. 'I'm sorry,' he intoned, meaningfully. 'Liz.'

Oh so now they must be quiet? Because of Liz? To hell with Liz! Jo let her own moans grow wilder. If they must love, let them love loudly. Let them walk with heads held high down this reckless path."

(There is a knock at the door.)

"Let them be caught, let them be punished, let them die even, but never again let these passions be muted."

LIZ. Jo?

(A jingle of keys.)

JO. "Let Liz bang on the door. She wouldn't stand to answer to Liz anymore. She didn't need to explain herself. She and Winston were in a war now, a war against a world that could not understand their love."

*(**LIZ** enters.)*

LIZ. Jo? Are you alright? What's going on? I knocked.

JO. Yes, and then you let yourself in.

LIZ. Yeah, I was worried. What's going on? I thought you were going to South Carolina. Josh is very upset.

JO. I just needed some space. I'm, actually, kind of in the middle of something.

LIZ. Okay, well I needed to check on you. Because Josh said you weren't answering your phone and because he said…

JO. What?

LIZ. Nothing. Look, I know he can be an asshole, but this is all temporary. You're going to get back on your feet.

JO. I know we are.

LIZ. You'll have your own place again. You won't have all this pressure. Let me check on that toilet by the way...

JO. It's fine.

LIZ. ...It's alright I'll just take a look, while I'm here...

(She goes into the bathroom.)

(Offstage.) You know I was thinking, about all the things you could write about. You were homecoming queen. Why don't you write about that? Or what about that trip to Mexico you went on.

JO. The trip to Mexico?

LIZ. *(Offstage.)* Yeah.

JO. That was in eleventh grade.

LIZ. *(Offstage.)* So? Wasn't there some funny thing that happened with, uh, a lost bus ticket?

JO. Liz, this is really not a good time.

LIZ. Why? What's going on?

*(**LIZ** notices two wine glasses.)*

What's that?

JO. What?

LIZ. Why are there two wine glasses out?

JO. I had a couple drinks.

LIZ. With two separate glasses, or with another separate person?

JO. This is my apartment. You can't just walk in here whenever you please.

LIZ. It's my house. Was someone here last night?

JO. It's none of your business. And we pay rent. /You can't just barge in here –

LIZ. You pay a family rate, because /we're family.

JO. Oh what, so I don't get privacy?

LIZ. No. Different rules apply. Now did you have a man here, in my house – that you admittedly pay rent to stay in – but still, in *my house*, there was a man here, who wasn't Josh??

JO. Yes.

LIZ. Did you sleep with this man?

JO. No. I mean… I did, but it wasn't real.

(**LIZ** *takes her time responding.*)

LIZ. Oh… It wasn't real… That's good. What a relief. What the hell are you talking about??

JO. Oh my god Liz. I really don't have time to explain this all to you but Winston is an actor.

LIZ. Winston? His name is Winston?

JO. No. That is his character's name. And he's been sent by the editors to help me move my story forward. Because I'm a writer, and that's how the process works. You think a book is written by just one person? Really, do you? No, it's an industry. You can't just work in a vacuum, you have to listen, you have to take suggestions.

LIZ. So this was your editors' idea? That you cheat on my brother?

JO. If you want to be reductive about it. I don't see it that way.

LIZ. How do you see it, Jo?

JO. I see it as doing my job. I love Josh, you know that. But I need to expand as a person, so I can write from a place of deeper experience.

LIZ. And what about his experience? What about your son?

JO. This is *for* my son. Don't try to twist this. This for Lincoln, more than anyone. I'm going to put him through college with this affair. And it's not just an affair. There's more to it. We're going to Colombia, and the story is going to just grow and grow.

LIZ. What?

(*The phone begins to ring.*)

JO. Look, I don't have to time to explain how this works.

LIZ. Jo, don't do this. You have a good life. Don't throw it away for some fling.

JO. I'm not throwing it away.

LIZ. Ten years you've been married. Ten years! You made a vow.

JO. And I will always honor that vow. On my personal time. But this is work. This is my career.

> (*She answers the phone.*)

Hello?

> (**SVEN** *and* **ANDREAS** *are on the line.*)

SVEN. Jo!

ANDREAS. It's Sven and Andreas.

JO. Oh hi. How are you? What's up?

LIZ. This is not right. You're not well.

SVEN. We're great. How are you, Jo? How's life?

JO. Getting pretty interesting, actually.

ANDREAS. Interesting, good!

JO. Yeah, I feel good about this current direction. Finally. Thanks for your help with that.

SVEN. Oh well, we just want to give you the support you need.

ANDREAS. You make it happen, Jo. You're the one with the talent.

SVEN. Yes, that's right.

LIZ. Jo, you're not well.

SVEN. Now look, Jo, we have some good news.

JO. What's that?

SVEN. We've been talking to some people about you and while we can't say anything definite now.

ANDREAS. There's definitely been some interest on the film side.

SVEN. We think there's a good chance we could sell the option rights to this thing.

ANDREAS. Probably even before it's released.

SVEN. Probably even before it's written. If you think things are taking a good tack.

JO. Oh my god, that's fantastic.

ANDREAS. Yeah.

SVEN. We thought you'd be excited.

> (**LIZ** *locks the doors to the apartment, as* **JO** *finishes packing with the phone in one hand.*)

Now look don't worry about this too much, but once these film people get involved…

LIZ. Jo, we're not done talking.

ANDREAS. They have their own agenda.

LIZ. Jo, look at me. You're having some kind of breakdown. You need to rest.

> (**LIZ** *takes* **JO**'s *suitcase.*)

ANDREAS. We don't want too many chefs /in the kitchen on this.

LIZ. You're going to stay here, and we are going to talk about this. Okay? This is not you.

SVEN. *(Simultaneous.)* Jo? Jo, is this a bad time?

LIZ. Someone's taking advantage of you.

JO. I'm taking advantage of myself!

> *(To phone.)*

I'm sorry.

> *(To* **LIZ**.*)*

Liz, give me my bag.

SVEN. Jo, what's happening?

JO. Nothing. My sister-in-law is here and she's trying to interfere. As usual.

SVEN. Oh yes. Liz.

ANDREAS. Liz Darum.

JO. Yeah. Liz Darum. What do you think the film people will think of her? As a character?

ANDREAS. Enhh.

SVEN. I mean, it's hard to say, but…

ANDREAS. Enh.

JO. I thought so.

(*JO and* **LIZ** *wrestle with the suitcase.* **JO** *puts down the phone to stop her while* **SVEN** *and* **ANDREAS** *continue on the line.*)

Give me the bag.

LIZ. No!

SVEN. ...You know, honestly, they probably won't get involved with character issues. The important thing with film is they want lots of action.

JO. Let go. Stop it!

(**JO** *struggles to get the suitcase away from* **LIZ.**)

SVEN. Now that doesn't mean you have to start living your life in three-act structure or anything.

ANDREAS. But if you did, that would save everyone a lot of work.

(*They laugh.*)

SVEN. Jo?	**LIZ.** Jo, you can't do this. You can't just hurt people like this.
ANDREAS. Jo? Are you there?	**JO.** I can't be afraid to hurt people. Not if I want to grow. I have a voice, Liz. Don't you understand? I have a voice. But what's the point of having a voice, if I don't have anything to say?

LIZ. Why do you need to say anything? Why can't you just be happy?

JO. Because it's a waste of my talent.

(**JO** *takes back the suitcase.*)

(*Picking up the phone.*) Hello? Are you still there?

(*Dial tone.*)

LIZ. Please, Jo. You're all he has.

JO. Of course, you would say that. You want me to stay here. You love that I live in your attic. You'd love it if

I stayed down here on your level. Happy. How are you happy? You work at the Bracelet Palace.

LIZ. I'm the manager. And yes, I'm happy. Why shouldn't I be happy? I have people who love me. And you have people who love you, too. Whatever this is, you don't need this. We love you. We love you.

JO. That kind of love is holding me back.

(She starts to go.)

LIZ. Jo, you're sick.

JO. Sick?? Or brave?? I'm making brave choices. Interesting choices. And someday, when you read my book, you'll identify with my character and wish you had the guts to do what she did.

(JO unlocks the door, and walks out.)

(Outside, snow is falling.)

(Lights out.)

11.

(Bogota, Colombia.)

(A halfway to scuzzy hotel room. **JO** *and* **WINSTON** *enter.* **JO** *is annoyed.)*

WINSTON. ...It wasn't that bad. The tour guide was so nice.

JO. Yes, he was very nice. I just thought it would be more interesting.

WINSTON. Well, I thought it was interesting. I've never been to a coffee plantation.

JO. And that would be fine, if something had happened there.

WINSTON. Well, a lot has happened. There's been a lot of history. Didn't you listen to what Luis was saying?

JO. It's not what I want that's important. It's what you want.

WINSTON. But you're not having fun.

JO. No, I'm having a lot of fun. I love being here with you, "in love." But...

WINSTON. What?

JO. In terms of what we do together, I hope you don't feel like you need to hold back.

WINSTON. Okay...

JO. There's nothing I'm afraid to do. *You* have ideas, I'm sure.

WINSTON. Now I'm afraid you don't like my ideas.

JO. *(Suggestive.)* I'm talking about bigger ideas. More adventurous ideas.

WINSTON. *(Confused, after a beat.)* Are you talking about, like, butt stuff?

JO. What?

WINSTON. Nothing.

JO. I'm talking about the book.

WINSTON. I'm sorry. I have trouble understanding you sometimes.

JO. I'm talking about the book. I think ideally this should be a story of redemption. Where Jo goes back to her family realizing that as wonderful as these experiences are, there is nothing she would trade for her family. But in order for that ending to be earned, she needs to go through something really deep.

WINSTON. …

JO. Or were you imagining something different?

WINSTON. Kind of. This is about redemption for you?

JO. Well, it's not for me to say what it's "about," but yeah, I hope so.

WINSTON. I think it's about redemption too.

JO. Really?

WINSTON. Yeah. I still can't believe that you're here. I'm so happy.

(He tries to kiss her. She recoils.)

What's wrong?

JO. Nothing.

WINSTON. Are you not into me anymore?

JO. No, I'm into you. But I already know how it feels to touch you, and I've already written that down, so.

WINSTON. So?

JO. So let's move the plot along. If all I got out of this affair was sex, then it's not much a book is it? I mean, it'd be a book but not *literature*. All we've been doing is walking around, eating things, and making love.

WINSTON. Sounds terrible.

JO. Are you making fun of me?

WINSTON. No!

JO. If you don't want to help me write my book, then what are you here for?

WINSTON. No, of course I want to help you.

JO. Then be a professional. Is there something you're not telling me?

WINSTON. No. What do you mean?

JO. Because you better not be holding back on the plot, just because you have personal feelings. That's not what this is.

WINSTON. I don't think in terms of plot.

JO. What do you think in terms of?

WINSTON. I'm just trying to live in the moment.

JO. But there's nothing happening!

WINSTON. Everything is happening. You just need to slow down and see it. I know you have a book to write, and I want you to be successful. I believe in you. I've always believed in you. But maybe – at least once or twice a day – you could stop thinking about how this is going to pay off somewhere down the line, and just live in the moment. With me. This is where the story is.

JO. Alright, I get it. I'm sorry. I shouldn't always try to think three steps ahead.

WINSTON. Yeah.

JO. And I trust you. I trust the process.

WINSTON. Good.

JO. And I'm really happy to be here with you. You're a wonderful character.

WINSTON. Thank you, baby.

JO. It's very exciting. But…

WINSTON. What?

JO. It would be great if I knew, not everything, but just the basic outline of what happens. Or at least, a timeline, so I know when I'm coming home.

WINSTON. I can't tell you that.

JO. Why not?

WINSTON. Because that's not how it works. I can't see the future. Maybe the story is you never go home.

> (*The hotel room phone rings.* WINSTON *goes to answer it.*)

JO. Never?

WINSTON. How could you? After we've known such bliss.

> *(On phone.)*

Si? …Digame…what? …How the fuck did you get this number…What…now? …No, it's just…no…it's fine… yeah…yeah…

> *(During the phone conversation, **JO**, sensing something important is happening, turns on her recorder.)*

JO. What is it?

WINSTON. It's my work. I'm sorry but I have to go out again.

JO. Now? It's late.

WINSTON. I'm sorry. It's sort of urgent. But I promise, it's going to get better. The story will pick up.

JO. Well, why don't you take me with you? It's time I got involved.

WINSTON. With what?

JO. With whatever the reason is we're here.

> *(She goes for his bag, begins opening it.)*

WINSTON. You don't want to be involved in this. It's not a very cool scene, believe me. Hey! HEY! Don't touch that!

> *(She steps back from the bag, startled. He takes it.)*

I'm sorry, I didn't mean to yell.

JO. It's alright. I get it –
I get it. You want to seem like you're protecting me. And it's suspenseful, and that's wonderful. But don't you think I've waited long enough?

WINSTON. For what?

JO. To find out. What you do. What this mysterious business of yours is?

WINSTON. It's not mysterious, it's just boring.

JO. *(Skeptical.)* Okay.

WINSTON. No, it is.

JO. Okay.

WINSTON. You really want to know?

JO. I want to know everything. Come on. What is it? Drugs? Guns?

WINSTON. Freezers.

JO. Organs. You smuggle organs.

WINSTON. I work for a company that sells industrial freezers. They require special servicing. We have contracts with the Carulla supermarket chain, and there's been a parts issue, so as part of the warranty agreement, I've had to come to oversee the repair in one of their locations.

JO. Ha ha.

WINSTON. Though it's in kind of a rough part of town, if that does anything for you. Here, I'll write down the address. They want to finish the job now, while there are less customers.

(He writes down an address.)

JO. Why are you writing that down?

WINSTON. Just in case there's an emergency.

JO. You want me to follow you there?

WINSTON. No no. Definitely not. It's dangerous. Especially for a woman alone.

JO. I see.

WINSTON. Just stay here. Relax. I'll be back in a few hours.

(He looks at her and doubts her, somehow.)

Seriously. It's dangerous.

JO. Understood.

WINSTON. You're going to stay here?

JO. Yes.

WINSTON. And not go here?

JO. To the address you wrote down on a piece of paper?

WINSTON. Yeah.

JO. Right. I definitely won't go there.

(**WINSTON**, *not believing her, starts to take back the piece of paper.*)

WINSTON. You know, you probably don't need this –

(**JO** *moves to stop him, reassuringly:*)

JO. No, no, I'd worry. Just leave it. I'm not going anywhere. I'll just go to bed, probably.

WINSTON. Probably?

JO. Definitely. I'm tired.

WINSTON. Okay. I'll be back in a few hours.

(*He starts to go.*)

JO. I'm so in love with you.

(**WINSTON** *looks at her. What is her deal? I mean, seriously. He leaves.* **JO** *dresses quickly, then follows him out.*)

12.

(The streets of Bogota.)

(JO speaks into her recorder.)

JO. As Jo traversed the dingy streets she did not feel lost, even though she had no idea where she was. Nor did she feel scared, even though her heart was pounding. Rather she felt exhilarated, out here, walking on the edge. It was clear from the expressions on the faces of the men who lined the streets that a gringa like she rarely came to *el barrio*, but what else could she do? She needed to know who Winston truly was. The address he left her seemed to be a supermarket. At least that was the front. Who knows what kind of double dealings went on in the back offices, between Winston and his associates. Jo paused before the automatic door, doubting herself. Maybe this was a mistake. Maybe she should enjoy the time they had together and not inquire too deeply into his shadowy second life. But no. If they were to be lovers, there could be no secrets between them. And Jo felt confident now, as she stepped inside the "supermarket," that she was strong enough to handle the truth.

(A few hours later, in the hotel room.)

(JO returns, WINSTON behind her.)

WINSTON. I don't understand why you're mad at me.

JO. Why? Why??

WINSTON. Yes.

JO. Because you lied to me!!

WINSTON. No, I didn't. When did I ever lie to you?

JO. You install freezers for a living!

WINSTON. That is exactly what I told you I did!

JO. I know! That's the problem!

WINSTON. Why? Why does that matter?

JO. Why does it matter?? Because I thought – I mean, do you even work in publishing?

WINSTON. No, I work in cooling technologies.

JO. Oh my god. So you're exactly what you claim to be??

WINSTON. Yes!

JO.

> So that means you're just
> some creepy
> loser who's been obsessed   **WINSTON.** Whoa.
> with me since
> high school, and I just…
> oh my god…oh my god…

WINSTON. I thought you said it was beautiful.

JO. Yeah, *as a story!*

WINSTON. Okay, so let me get this straight – I think I have this figured out, but let me just make sure – you think I was sent by your publishers to help perform some kind of fantasy for you to write about? Is that what you think?

JO. Yes.

WINSTON. Because other people don't have anything better to do than help you live out your little fantasies – but they aren't allowed to have any real feelings themselves because that would be *creepy*??

JO. Basically. I mean, when you put it that way it sounds crazy.

WINSTON. I don't know what to say.

JO. Never mind, it is crazy. I'm crazy…

WINSTON. I didn't say that.

JO. …I'm not a good enough writer for anyone to go to all this trouble, of…of…of… *(Gesturing at the phenomenon of time unfolding.)*

WINSTON. What?

JO. I thought you were this amazing actor.

> *(He doesn't know what to say. She begins to pack her things.)*

WINSTON. Wait. You're going?

JO. Yes.

WINSTON. Wait, Jo.

> (*He moves toward her.*)

JO. Don't touch me.

WINSTON. Jo, wait just listen.

JO. What?

WINSTON. Sometimes people invent stories. To help them.

JO. What?

WINSTON. Maybe you invented this story in your mind, so that you would have a reason to do what you really want to do.

JO. Which is what?

WINSTON. Which is be with me.

JO. I don't even know who you are.

WINSTON. Isn't that what makes it exciting? And whatever you might have thought about the circumstances that brought us together, the fact is you feel something for me.

JO. No.

WINSTON. You do. You can't pretend that what we went through wasn't, intermittently, something real.

JO. It doesn't matter.

WINSTON. Why?

JO. Because now I know the truth.

WINSTON. You think you know the truth. There is more to me.

JO. I don't think so.

WINSTON. Yes there is. I am layered and rich. Full of secrets and…reversals. I mean what if I told you – I can't believe I'm doing this – what if told you I do work for the publishers?

JO. You don't. You don't. You already said you don't.

WINSTON. Because that's my job. Jo, I'm an actor. An amazing actor.

JO. I don't believe you.

WINSTON. I'll take that as a compliment. I wouldn't believe me, either. But that doesn't change the fact that you still have a book to write. And they're making a movie.

JO. *(Caught offguard.)* How do you know they're making a movie?

WINSTON. Exactly. How do I know that?

JO. How *do* you know that?

WINSTON. I'm not supposed to talk about it. We're not supposed to talk about any of this. Or did you think Sven and Andreas wanted a book where you talk about *your process* as you go along. Writing about writing. Oh, that'll be a big success. Wake up. Who do you think you're working for?

JO. How do you know Sven and Andreas?

WINSTON. It's not just your story, Jo. A lot of people have put a lot of time and money into this project.

JO. I mentioned them. You heard me mention them.

WINSTON. They mentioned themselves, when they hired me ten years and twenty-three titles ago. And not once, in all that time, have I once broken character.

JO. You work for a freezer company.

WINSTON. *My character* works for a freezer company. Or did you think we had to insert a drug dealer to make your narrative compelling? Ugh. I'm sick of playing drug dealers. We're trying to do something different with this one. Your problem is you have too many preconceptions. The book doesn't happen until you forget you're writing it. Here. Go ahead and call Sven and Andreas if you don't believe me.

(He picks up the hotel phone, offers it to her.)

You don't believe me? Call Sven and Andreas.

(She takes the phone and begins dialing.)

They might deny it at first, but that's because they really
don't like to go meta. But they'll cop to it if it keeps you
on the project.

JO. I need a phone card.

WINSTON. Here.

> *(He gives her a phone card.)*

We were about to go to the next chapter, too. I was
almost done at the supermarket.

JO. How do I…?

WINSTON. Dial nine to get out. Then the number on the
card. Then wait for the prompt, and dial the number
you want to dial.

> *(A beat, as she dials.)*

They might not be there. It's late.

JO. *(On phone.)* This is Jo Darum. May I speak to Sven or
Andreas, please?

WINSTON. But anyway, we have a whole next part.

JO. *(On phone.)* Okay. Can you please have them return?
I'm in room nine at the Casa del Sol in Bogota. In
Colombia, yes. Thank you.

> *(**JO** hangs up.)*

WINSTON. There is a plan. Even if you can't see it.

JO. Tell me it.

WINSTON. What?

JO. Tell me what happens in the story. If there's a plan.

WINSTON. Well, it's not all filled in yet.

JO. *(Turning away.)* Then it's not a plan.

WINSTON. *(Saving it.)* Okay, fine. You want to know? It
won't be a surprise if I tell you now, but fine, fine.
In the next chapter, after we get through this whole
misunderstanding, we were going to rent a car.

JO. Oh wow. A car. That's really impressive.

WINSTON. Are you going to listen?

> *(**JO** gestures to go ahead.)*

We were going to drive out of town up to the mountains.
Up to this cloud forest. But not the normal way, on the
trail where all the tourists go, because that would be
boring, so that's not what happens. What happens is.
Um.

*(A beat. He seems lost, but will refocus moving
forward, the vision sharpening.)*

JO. What?

WINSTON. We were going to go to this village. We were
going to go to this little village, okay? The premise
would be we're stopping to get some water and fruit,
on our way to the cloud forest, like as if everything
would be normal. But then, while I'm buying the stuff,
you would see this woman with a baby in a sling. The
sling is made from this blue plastic material that looks
like an Ikea bag, and you think that's just such a nice
detail, so you start to talk to her. And she speaks English
and is very sweet and, unlike all these other people
here trying to sell us arts and crafts and whatever, she
doesn't want anything from you. Because she's an actor.
Ideally, you wouldn't know that. But anyway, what was
going to happen was, she was going to invite us to her
house for lunch. And we would accept because it seems
like a chance to have a really authentic experience. So
we would go sit in this lady's little cinderblock house
with a corrugated tin roof and eat boiled chicken.
And eventually – I don't know her whole script – but
she was going to say something about how there is a
"secret way" up to the cloud forest, not for gringos. So
obviously you would be like, "We want to go that way."
But she would be like, "No, it's sacred," but then I
would give her money and she would be like, "It's right
over there." And she's pointing to just, like, some area
behind her house – which feels a little shady to me, at
least that's how I'd play it, since we're just in this dirty
little village in the middle of nowhere – and I'd be
like, "I don't know," and you'd be like, "We have to do
this." And I'd be like, "Nobody even knows we're here.

What if somebody fucking kills us?" And you'd be like, "Yeah…but what if they *don't?*" …So we would leave the car and we start walking. A couple of actors playing kids would follow us, and dogs. And then there's more dogs and kids. It's like *The Wizard of Oz,* just this gathering group of friends except we're not friends and actually we make each other uncomfortable. This one kid keeps getting really close and at one point you think he's pricked you with something, but you can't tell, and you don't want to make accusations, it's not even your country. Eventually, we enter the jungle, and the kids turn back. Then most of the dogs turn back. And then the trail starts to get steep. And by now there's only one dog following us, a black one. His name is Pele. He's mangy and missing one eye and just wonderful – I wish he had a bigger part in the story but he's only there for that one section and then he's gone. And we're alone in the jungle, walking this amazing trail that wasn't even there a few months ago, that we made for you. A brand new trail, made to look like it's hundreds of years old. And in the jungle there's all these birds. And a monkey. And a type of jungle rat called an agouti – we like to fill the world with animals, so our writers can use them as symbols to express their inner lives. We keep walking, higher, until we reach the cloud forest. It's not actually the cloud forest, it's just a section of jungle we've filled with mist, but it doesn't matter, it's beautiful and mysterious. Eventually, the way it was supposed to go, you would lose me in the mist. And you would have this moment of panic. You'd call out, "Winston? Where are you, my love?" And you'd get no response. You don't know where I am and you feel afraid. You start to run, but you can barely see three feet ahead of you – we've pumped too much mist into the jungle! – It's really over the top, but we wanted it to feel unreal. But it also makes it hard to see and, you trip. You trip off the edge of the trail we made for you. You tumble down a slope, over wet plants, you can't stop yourself, you're falling right toward the edge of this cliff. But at the last minute you grab onto something, a root, which we've reinforced with cable. You're hanging off the edge of this cliff, feet dangling. Below you is a river, about eighty feet down. I know. It sounds dangerous but every possible precaution would have been taken. Life guards would be standing by and I'm confident we could have pulled it off without a hitch. I would have come scrambling down to the edge of the cliff. You would have seen me emerging from the mist. I would have pulled you up into my arms. You would have sobbed. And I'm just, like, comforting you. It takes you a while to calm down. Your heart is beating so fast. So fast. Like a hummingbird in your chest. Or a fast hammer. I don't know. It's not my job to describe it... It's just my job to hold you.

> *(A long beat.)*

JO. And then what?

WINSTON. Then I, speaking as me, speaking as my character, I'd say, "We can go back if you want to." And what do you think your character would have said?

JO. No.

WINSTON. That's right. Because that's the kind of person you are in the story we planned for you. Not a quitter... you want to see the top of the mountain. And we only turned on all that mist so that when you see, it's all the more magnificent. And when we get to the top, it's just...wow. Mountains. Sky. Sea. Actually, you shouldn't be able to see the sea, but it felt more spectacular to put that in too, so there it is. It's majestic. You start to cry. We release more birds. You cry harder. "Never leave me again," you say. "I won't," I say.

> *(**WINSTON** gets his duffle bag as **JO** stares off at the picture he has painted.)*

We'll never be apart, ever again. "It's so beautiful," you would say. "It's the most beautiful thing I've ever seen. Winston, isn't it the most beautiful thing you've ever seen?"

*(WINSTON takes out an engagement ring and gets
on his knees. She doesn't notice immediately.)*

And I don't say anything at first. So you repeat yourself.
"Winston, isn't it the most beautiful thing you've ever
seen." And then you turn around and see me, like this.
And then I say, "No, *you* are the most beautiful thing
I've ever seen."

JO. What are you doing?

WINSTON. The book will be an international best seller.
It will be translated into thirty-nine languages. They'll
make it into a movie. You'll be played by Jennifer
Lawrence and I'll be played by Bradley Cooper. The
audience will want us to be together.

JO. No.

WINSTON. They'll laugh when you laugh, they'll cry when
you cry, and in that way, these moments we share,
will take on a life, a life that lives beyond us. And in
that way, *we* live beyond us. We live on that mountain
forever.

JO. No, we don't.

WINSTON. We can! We just need to finish the story.

JO. *(Certain.)* We're in different stories.

(A beat.)

WINSTON. Well that's just one version of it.

JO. I have to go home. I have a husband. I have a kid…

WINSTON. Wait, Jo, we're so close. I can tweak the… What
can I do? How can I be the man you need me to be?

JO. You can't. I never even saw you as a man. You were just
a device.

WINSTON. A device?

*(A pause. JO goes to the phone, dials JOSH's cell
number.)*

JO. I can't write about this. What I write about has to be
real.

(A beat.)

WINSTON. Alright.

> (**WINSTON** *walks abruptly out of the room.* **JO** *connects with* **JOSH**.)

JOSH. Hello?

JO. Josh? It's me.

> (*A beat.*)

Josh?

JOSH. Yes?

JO. How is Myrtle Beach?

JOSH. I'm not in Myrtle Beach, I'm home.

JO. Josh…

JOSH. Are you in Colombia?

JO. Yes, how did you know?

JOSH. Oh I could just tell by the reception. It sounded Colombian to me.

JO. Josh, I'm so sorry. I made a mistake –

JOSH. Oh did you?

JO. I was confused. I thought they wanted me to do this.

JOSH. Right. Well, you hear what you want to hear, don't you?

JO. I thought they wanted me to be in a romance.

JOSH. They?

JO. My editors.

JOSH. Oh I see. And did they tell you this romance should be with someone else?

JO. No.

JOSH. No, so you just assumed that?

JO. I was confused. I thought I needed to do something new.

JOSH. Why?

JO. To keep things interesting. I thought they might think you were…

JOSH. What? I was *what*? An unlikable character? What about you, Jo? What makes you think you're likable?

There's nothing that kills a book faster than an unlikable main character. You think you're likable for abandoning us *so you can have something to write about?*

JO. I know you don't believe me but everything I did I did for us.

JOSH. Oh come on. You really think I'm going to believe that?

JO. I made a mistake. We've both made mistakes.

JOSH. I didn't make my mistakes on purpose. You did this because this is what you wanted. You. Admit it. Admit it –

JO. You're right. I wanted to leave.

JOSH. Why?

JO. Because I wanted to see.

JOSH. You wanted to see what?

JO. I wanted to see if losing you would make me want you again.

JOSH. And? Did it?

JO. Yes.

JOSH. Well, that's good. I'm happy you went on such a fulfilling journey of personal self discovery. I just don't know how to explain it to our son.

(**WINSTON** *returns, listening in.*)

JO. Can I speak to him?

JOSH. I don't think that's a good idea.

JO. Please Josh. I want to come home.

JOSH. I don't know how to do that now. In fact, I don't think it's healthy for us to be around you for a while.

JO. No Josh please. I want to come home.

JOSH. You can stay at a hotel with your book money.

JO. I don't want to stay at a hotel.

JOSH. Well, you don't get to make this decision. I hope you enjoy the rest of your trip.

JO. Josh, don't –

JOSH. …I hope you end up becoming a really interesting person.

> *(He hangs up.)*

JO. Josh? …Hello?

> *(She looks to see **WINSTON** there.)*

WINSTON. Was that Josh?

JO. Yes.

WINSTON. I just want you to know I don't mind being a device. I'm here to help. I can still help you write your romance.

JO. No, you can't.

WINSTON. Why?

JO. You just can't. Anyhow, they don't publish romances. They publish ordeals. I'm such an idiot.

WINSTON. Well we could make it an ordeal. I can help make it harder. Whatever you want. What do you want? More conflict? We can go back to that bad part of town.

JO. What's going to happen there?

WINSTON. I don't know. Maybe you'll get attacked by drug dealers, and I'll save you.

JO. It wouldn't make sense for me to be saved. At this point, I deserve to have something horrible happen to me. That's the kind of book they publish. And that's what I deserve.

WINSTON. I can help you.

> *(She looks at him. He looks at her. A moment of unpleasant understanding.)*

I know what kind of books you mean.

> *(He moves toward her.)*

And if you want me to do something, I can do something.

JO. I don't want you to do anything.

WINSTON. You do though. I can tell. This book means a lot to you.

JO. There's not going to be a book. I'm not going to write about any of this.

WINSTON. Don't say that. Don't give up on yourself. Together, we can tell a story worth telling.

JO. Get off of me!

WINSTON. This is what you want, isn't it? You want to go through something real.

JO. Get the fuck off of me!

WINSTON. No one else would be willing to do this. It's because I understand you, in a way Josh will never understand you.

> (**WINSTON** *forces himself on her and covers her mouth.*)

Think of the book.

> (*He pushes her against the wall face first, while unbuttoning his pants.*)

Love waits. Great title.

> (*She bites his hand. He shouts as* **JO** *tries to escape. He pursues her as she leaps over the bed. He grabs her foot and begins pulling her toward him.*)

> (**JO** *takes the phone off the side table and smashes* **WINSTON** *in the face. He is knocked down.*)

> (*She jumps on him with the phone and brings it down on his head, hard. And then again. And then again…until he is dead.*)

> (*She sits there, panting and exhausted. Several beats, then the phone, now covered in blood, rings.*)

> (**JO**, *after a few moments, answers it.*)

JO. Hello?

SVEN. Jo, it's Sven Kandetty.

ANDREAS. And me.

SVEN. And Andreas. How are you, Jo? How's Colombia? … Jo? Are you there?

JO. Yes.

SVEN. Is everything going well?

JO. No.

SVEN. Oh, well it can't always be fun.

ANDREAS. From great pain comes great art.

SVEN. That's our slogan. Now look, Jo, we were so happy to hear from you. We have something we need to tell you.

JO. What?

SVEN. Oh, it's nothing bad, it's just we passed on *Dragonscape* to the movie people.

ANDREAS. And much to our surprise…

SVEN. Much to our delight…

ANDREAS. They really responded to it.

SVEN. We think they're going to make an offer… Isn't that wonderful? Jo?

ANDREAS. They're going to turn *Dragonscape* into a movie.

JO. *(Baffled, horrified.)* But what about the memoir? What about my real story? I thought you only dealt with stories that were real.

SVEN. Well, we do. That's true. But…

ANDREAS. People are looking for all different things.

JO. No no no. I came to Colombia because I thought this was what you wanted!

SVEN. Well it's not what we want that's important…

ANDREAS. It's your book.

JO. I thought this was what you wanted, so I came here with this man, and then he forced himself on me and I killed him.

SVEN. Who?

JO. Winston! He forced himself on me and I killed him. That's the story. So what do you think? Is that a book? Is that the kind of thing people will find interesting?

SVEN. Well, Jo… I think it's important to be honest.

JO. Yes?

ANDREAS. It sounds a little dark.

(Lights out.)

13.

(Two years later. Home in New Jersey. There are boxes out, as JO *and* JOSH *are in the process of moving.)*

*(*JO *enters with* JOSH *and* LINCOLN*. They are returning from a movie premiere and dressed up.)*

LINCOLN. I liked it.

JO. Oh, I don't know.

LINCOLN. Except the dragons were too big.

JO. Exactly. The dragons were too big. But that's okay. I don't even have a problem with that. It's that they changed the relationships. Phaemora isn't in love with Boaboar, she looks after him.

JOSH. Well, I thought it was amazing. Just to see all those characters, like, played by actors that I recognize, wow. Blew my mind.

JO. I guess it was entertaining.

*(*JOSH *takes* JO *in his arms as* LIZ *enters, looking at her phone.)*

LIZ. Oh my god, you guys. The reviews are coming out.

JO. Oh no…

LINCOLN. What do they say?

JOSH. No. No reviews. It's not important what other people think. All that's important is what you think.

LINCOLN. But I want to know if I'm right or not.

JOSH. No. Anyhow, we don't have time. We're just stopping by to change before dinner.

LIZ. Come on, kiddo.

*(*LIZ *and* LINCOLN *exit, as* JO *steps into the side room to change.* JOSH *sees a message on the answering machine.)*

JO. Thank you. I don't need to hear all that. Not that it matters. It's not my movie.

JOSH. It is your movie. It's your story.

JO. *(Modest.)* The story is generic. It's alright. I sold it. We did it.

JOSH. You did it. Took you long enough. I can't wait to get the hell outta here.

JO. Are you sure, you won't miss this place, just a little? You might feel nostalgic some day.

JOSH. That's a risk I'm willing to take.

> *(****JOSH**** goes to the phone machine where a light is blinking.)*

Oh, we got a message.

JO. Hm?

> *(He presses the button. The familiar voices of* **SVEN** *and* **ANDREAS** *are heard.)*

SVEN. Jo!

ANDREAS. It's Sven and Andreas.

SVEN. Just want to congratulate you on your big day, Jo.

ANDREAS. So exciting.

JOSH. What the hell?

JO. Why are they calling on the landline?

SVEN. Look, Jo, we're sorry to be calling on the landline.

ANDREAS. But we couldn't seem to reach you at your old number.

SVEN. Not that we blame you for changing it.

ANDREAS. After all the press last year from what happened in Colombia.

SVEN. But you know, any press is good press.

ANDREAS. You're a star, Jo!

SVEN. Just don't forget the little people.

> *(They laugh.)*

JOSH. These clowns never give up. Alright if I kill this?

> *(****JO**** nods. ****JOSH**** is about to stop the message.)*

SVEN. Now look, Jo we're looking forward to speaking with you about your manuscript, whenever you get a chance.

JOSH. What the hell?

JO. It's alright, you can delete it.

JOSH. What manuscript?

SVEN. But look, we know you're probably out with your family.

ANDREAS. Or probably about to go out with your family.

JO. It's nothing.

(**JO** *walks to the answering machine and...*)

SVEN. Possibly you just came home from the movie premiere and are just changing before you –

(*...stops the message.*)

JOSH. I thought we talked about this. You're not seriously thinking about letting them publish a book about what happened.

JO. They gave me an advance. I never delivered.

JOSH. We don't need the money. You can get other work now. It's not worth it.

JO. I know, but I had already been writing everything down, just for myself. But then they asked me if they could read it, so I thought why not...

JOSH. I thought you weren't talking to them anymore.

JO. It's not their fault what happened. But if it bothers you, I won't. Not if it embarrasses you.

JOSH. It's not about being embarrassed. I just don't think you should dig up the past. You want people to always associate you with what happened with you and him?

JO. There are people who think I wasn't attacked. I wanted to set the record straight.

JOSH. If you start talking about it, you're only going to raise more questions. I just want things to be normal for us.

JO. You're right. I'll tell them I don't want it published.

(*She moves for the phone.*)

I'll give them the advance back. I'll call them right now.

JOSH. You don't need to call them right now...

JO. No, it's okay…

JOSH. It's late…

JO. They don't sleep. I'd rather tell them now and be done with it.

JOSH. Well. Alright then.

JO. Josh. I love you. Never change.

JOSH. I won't.

> *(**JOSH** leaves. **JO** dials **SVEN** and **ANDREAS**.)*

SVEN. Hello?

JO. Hello. It's Jo Darum.

SVEN. Jo. Hold on, let me get Andreas.

> *(**ANDREAS** immediately appears on the phone somewhere else.)*

ANDREAS. Hello, I'm here.

JO. Hi.

ANDREAS. Hi, Jo! How was the premiere?

JO. It was fine. Listen, I just wanted to tell you guys, about the book, I don't want to publish.

ANDREAS. Oh no…

SVEN. No, you don't?

JO. Yeah, I would just rather…not dig up the past.

SVEN. Oh. Well, that's such a shame, Jo. We love your book.

JO. You do?

SVEN. Oh yes.

ANDREAS. Well, we have questions…

SVEN. Yes…

JO. About what? I mean, it doesn't matter. I don't want to expose myself. Or my family.

SVEN. Oh well, that's a shame. That's just what we love about the book, Jo. How much you exposed yourself.

ANDREAS. Yes, you're very naked in the book.

SVEN. Naked in a good way.

ANDREAS. Yes. Well, for the most part.

JO. What does that mean?

ANDREAS. Well, it doesn't matter now does it? Not if you don't want to finish it.

SVEN. She doesn't need to finish it now. With all that Hollywood money ha ha.

ANDREAS. We're so happy about that.

SVEN. And if all you're looking for is a paycheck, then you have found your calling.

JO. That's not all I'm looking for.

SVEN. Oh?

JO. No.

SVEN. *(Certain.)* We know. Because otherwise you wouldn't have written this manuscript to begin with. You wouldn't have shown it to us. You to us. Unless you wanted to be seen.

ANDREAS. Being seen is even better than having something to say.

SVEN. We think you can do both.

ANDREAS. Possibly even at the same time, Jo.

SVEN. Like someone who can pat their head while rubbing their bellies.

ANDREAS. You're gifted.

JO. You really think so?

ANDREAS. Oh yes.

JO. Alright, well, what are your questions then?

SVEN. Well… I suppose our main concern is the ending.

JO. What's wrong with the ending?

SVEN. Well, we love the basic idea, of a happy ending, you come home to your family, everything's nice la la la. We're just wondering…

ANDREAS. Is it earned?

SVEN. Yes…

JO. Of course it's earned. She went through something so traumatic. It was shattering. It made her realize how much she loves her family and that there was nothing worth sacrificing them for ever again.

SVEN. Well…

ANDREAS. That's a nice idea.

SVEN. It feels a little theoretical /at this point.

LIZ. *(Entering.)* Jo?

JO. *(To LIZ.)* Just one moment.

SVEN. Basically everything that happened to Jo she brought on herself.

ANDREAS. Which is fine, for a first draft.

LIZ. Jo?

JO. *(Irritated.)* What?

LIZ. Did Lincoln come back up here?

SVEN. Jo? Remember how we told you we liked the character of Lincoln?

(Lights out.)

End of Play